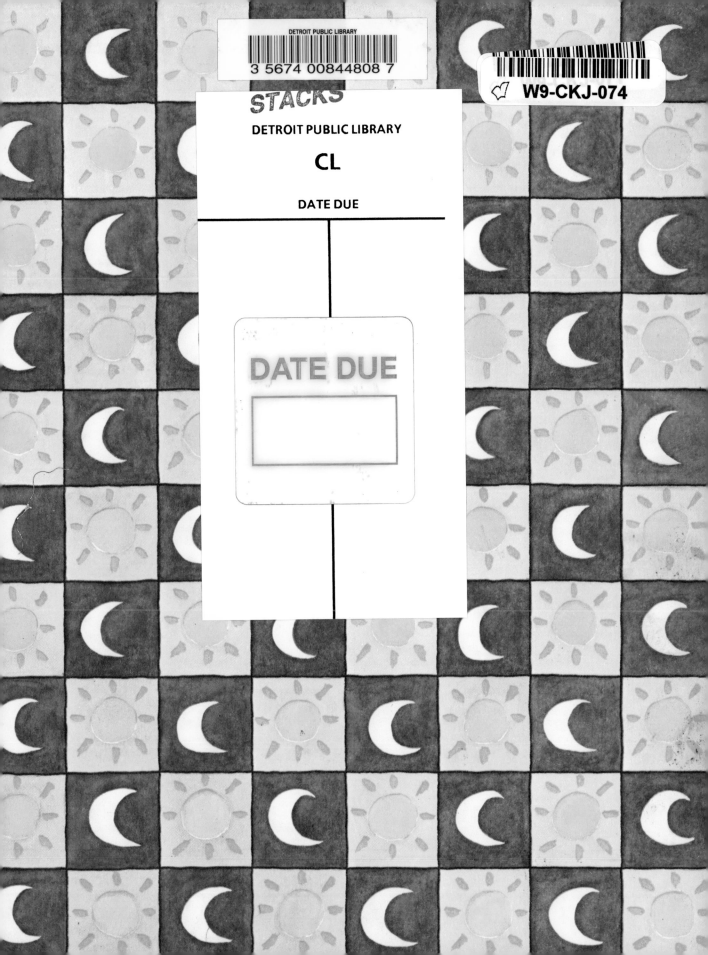

THE TOMORROW BOOK

by Doris Schwerin
pictures by Karen Gundersheimer

PANTHEON BOOKS · NEW YORK

Library of Congress Cataloging in Publication Data
Schwerin, Doris. The tomorrow book.
Summary: Describes some of the nice things that tomorrow can bring from
a sunny day to new skills. [1. Time—Fiction]   I. Gundersheimer, Karen, ill.
II. Title. PZ7.S412635To   1984   [E]   82-12504
ISBN 0-394-85459-4   ISBN 0-394-95459-9 (lib. bdg.)

For Benjamin who helps me remember

D.S.

Love to my parents

K.G.

Is it dark outside?

Then it's nighttime!

Where are the children?

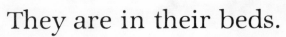They are in their beds.

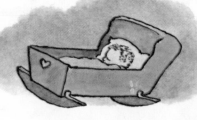

It's time to say "Good night" and close your eyes.

When you wake up and say "Good morning!"
it will be TOMORROW.

"Hello day! Hello light!

I want breakfast!"

TOMORROW you can do lots of things there wasn't time to do today.

Run again…Hide again…

Climb up a hill...or down a hill...

Sing a new song that goes,

PUM-DE-DUM, PUM-DE-DUM, DOODLE-Y DOODLE-Y DAY!

Maybe TOMORROW you will go to the market
to buy a loaf of bread to make sandwiches,
and maybe some crunchy carrots and
juicy oranges and yellow bananas and
grapes that go "pop" when you bite them.

Maybe TOMORROW you will blow bubbles
and watch the bubbles float up and up
in the air, and down and down
until you can't see them anymore.

What happened today?
Did it rain, or was the sun shining?
Did you play inside and build a tower of blocks?
TOMORROW you can build another tower,
even higher, and yell "Zowie!" when it falls!

Did you lose a toy today?
A car, a bear, a very small ball?
Maybe you'll find it TOMORROW,
under a bed, or behind a chair, or anywhere.

TOMORROW could be the day you learn
how to do something all by yourself.

Maybe you'll meet a new friend TOMORROW.
You'll say, "Hi! What's *your* name?"
And your new friend will say, "Hi! My name
is Jody."

Maybe your new friend's name will be

Sheba or Francie, Maria or Bettie.

Jenna?  Rooley?  Pooley?

Or maybe it will be

Johnny or Chang, Daniel or Benjy.

 Mikey? 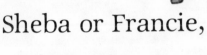 Spikey?

Maybe it will be José.

Did something make you cry today?
Did you bang things and throw things around?
Did you get a bump on your head?
Or a scratch on your finger?

Well, during the night while you're sleeping,
maybe your bump will go down,
maybe your scratch will begin to heal,
and TOMORROW everything will
feel *much* better.

You might even smile from morning till night...
TOMORROW.

Here are some kisses for today and TOMORROW...

all for you!

DORIS SCHWERIN lives in New York City. She is a composer, a playwright and the author of the widely acclaimed *Diary of a Pigeon Watcher*, *Leanna* (a novel in six movements), and a forthcoming book entitled *Rainbow Walkers*. *The Tomorrow Book* was written for her grandson, Benjamin, when he was two and was pondering the question of future time, which at that age means "tomorrow."

KAREN GUNDERSHEIMER is a well-known illustrator whose pictures have distinguished many books for children, including Sally Whittman's *A Special Trade*, Jane Feder's *Beany* and her own *Happy Winter*, all ALA Notable Books. She has also collaborated with James Skofield on *Nightdances*, and with Charlotte Zolotow on *Some Things Go Together*. She lives in Philadelphia with her husband, a professor of history at the University of Pennsylvania. They have two sons, Josh and Ben.